RUPERT

and the
FUNNY
JOKE MAN

CARNIVAL

R upert and his pal, Bill
Badger, are out playing on
Nutwood Common one day when
they hear a loud wailing coming
from a blackberry bush. The
chums turn in surprise and see an
oddly-dressed figure with tears
running down his face.

'Why, whatever is the matter?'
asks Rupert.

The strange figure is dressed like a court jester in a bright red and white silk suit with bells fastened to his jacket.

'Boo-hoo-hoo,' he cries. 'I must have dropped it somewhere and now I can't find it anywhere.'

'What have you lost?' asks Rupert.

The little man blinks at him tearfully. 'Why, my sense of humour, of course!'

His lips begin to tremble. 'I have to make up lots of jokes to go in the crackers at Christmas, but I can't think of *any* without my sense of humour.'

'Cheer up,' says Rupert kindly. 'Bill and I know plenty of jokes you can put in your Christmas crackers.'

The jester tugs his arm. 'Come with me to the Cracker Factory now,' he pleads. 'We must start straight away.'

He lifts aside a tangle of branches and ducks into the middle of the blackberry bush.

'It's this way and through the door.'

The chums follow the jester and arrive at a small clearing deep inside the bush. At one end is an odd-shaped yellow door. 'In here,' beckons the jester.

He leads them along a narrow
passage to a store-room piled
high with boxes of crackers!

Rupert and Bill stare around in
amazement. Then they are
bundled into a lift and whirred
upwards.

When the lift opens, they step into a brightly-lit workshop crowded with benches heaped with hats, novelties, crêpe paper and card.

At the far end, seated behind a high raised desk, is a cross-looking fairy. 'Well,' she says sternly, 'did you find it?'

The jester hurries towards her.

'I looked everywhere, I really did, and I *am* going back to look again, but meanwhile,' – he glances anxiously at Rupert and Bill – 'these two say they know lots of jokes and can help us.'

'Indeed?' The fairy puts on a pair of tiny silver spectacles and peers at the two pals. 'You don't *look* as if you know any good jokes,' she says doubtfully. 'You aren't wearing the right clothes at all.'

She sighs wearily. 'If *he* hadn't lost his sense of humour somewhere, none of this would be necessary.'

'I'm sure he hasn't *really* lost it,' protests Rupert. 'It can't fall out of your pocket like a penny or a key, you know. It's not that sort of thing.'

'Not that sort of thing?' The fairy looks furious. 'Do you mean we've spent all this time looking for something that *isn't lost at all*?'

'Oh dear,' thinks Rupert, 'I wish I hadn't said that!'

Then an idea strikes him.
'Perhaps there's a way we can
help with the crackers and also
get his sense of humour back,' he
says. 'Tell us a joke, Bill.'

'Right-o,' says Bill. 'What lion never moves?'

Rupert shakes his head.

'A dandelion!' chuckles Bill.

'That's very good,' cries the little jester. 'I must write that down.'

Bill grins. 'And did you hear about the boy who spilt glue over his maths book and got stuck in the middle of a sum?'

'Oh, I say!' gulps the jester, scribbling frantically.

'And what do you call . . . ?

'Hang on a minute,' interrupts the jester. 'I've just thought of one myself – what game does the wind play?'

Bill looks blank.

'Draughts, of course,' chortles
the little man.

Rupert gives a shout of glee. 'There – your sense of humour has come back. I knew it would.'

The jester blinks in surprise. 'So it has. Those jokes of Bill's have put me in a joking mood myself.'

'In that case,' says the fairy, actually smiling a little herself, 'perhaps we can all get back to work.'

The jester turns to Rupert. 'You knew exactly what to do to get my sense of humour back. However can I thank you?'

'By putting lots of good jokes in our Christmas crackers,' smiles Rupert.

And, of course, that's exactly what he *did*. Rupert and Bill will be watching out for them when they pull their crackers on Christmas Day – don't forget to do the same!

Carnival
An imprint of the Children's Division
of the Collins Publishing Group
8 Grafton Street, London W1X 3LA

First published by Dragon Books 1986
Published by Carnival 1989

Written by Len Collis
Illustrated by Jon Davis
Copyright © The Nutwood Press 1986
Copyright © Title and character of Rupert Bear,
Express Newspapers plc 1986

ISBN 0 00 194458 4

Printed & bound in Great Britain by
PURNELL BOOK PRODUCTION LIMITED
a member of BPCC plc